Anonymous

Through the Year : Spring, Summer, Autumn, Winter

Anonymous

Through the Year : Spring, Summer, Autumn, Winter

ISBN/EAN: 9783744756273

Printed in Europe, USA, Canada, Australia, Japan

Cover: Foto ©Andreas Hilbeck / pixelio.de

More available books at **www.hansebooks.com**

Through
the year.

The original Verses are by
E. Nesbit Caris Brooke, Theo. Gift and C. Mannering.
Thanks are due to Eirikr Magnússon Esq., for permission to use the
translations from Runeberg,
and to Austin Dobson, Esq., for permission to use,
"Love in Winter."

The Illustrations are by
L. Bernard Hall, G. H. Thompson, A. Wilde Parsons, Julius Luz,
Robert Ellice Mack, A. M. Clausen, W. G. Addison,
G. W. Harvey, George Clausen, Lizzie Lawson, H. Whatley, H. Bannerman,
Mary E. Butler, G. H. Thompson and Giacomelli.

and the book is produced and printed
by Ernest Nister of Nuremberg.

Throu

The year

Spring. Summer. Autumn. Wint

New York
E. P. Dutton & Company
31 West Twenty-Third St

SPRING.

THIS day Dame Nature seemed in love:
The lusty sap began to move:
Fresh juice did stir th' embracing vines,
And birds had drawn their valentines.
The jealous trout that low did lie,
Rose at a well-dissembled fly;
Already were the eaves possess'd
With the swift pilgrim's daubèd nest:
The groves already did rejoice,
In Philomel's triumphing voice:
The showers were short, the weather mild,
The morning fresh, the evening smiled.
Joan takes her neat-rubbed pail, and now
She trips to milk the sand-red cow.
The fields and gardens were beset
With tulips, crocus, violet;
And now, though late, the modest rose
Did more than half a blush disclose.
Thus all looks gay and full of cheer,
To welcome the new-liveried year.

SIR H. WOTTON.

*A*WAY and away with the breezes
  At play with the young budding boughs,
    Tossing the plumes of the larches,
  Bending the green birchen arches,
    Telling the pine trees what March is,
  The maddest and gladdest carouse!

I.

Away with the white cloudlets flying
  In scattered wreaths over the blue:
    Running and romping and chasing,
    Sunshine and shadow displacing,
    Oh! sweet fairy lover, what racing,
Ere springtime is over, we'll do!

We'll hie to the moss-mantled forest,
  And pinch every bud as we pass,
    The leaflets will leap out to greet us,
    The crocus spring upward to meet us,
    The shy little daisies entreat us
To kiss their pink lips thro' the grass.

The hill-sides are breaking in blossom,
  The daffodil romps on the lea,
    Her kirtlet of gold she is sporting,
    While pretty red nettle goes courting;
    And "lords" their fair "ladies" escorting,
  Stand sceptred and stately to see.

II.

The brown lark is trilling and thrilling
    In rivers of song from on high;
      The linnets are chirping and cheeping,
      The thrushes their love-trysts are keeping,
      The wee, woolly lambkins are leaping
    For joy that the Spring-time is nigh.

It is come! It is here! It is with us,
    Born of strong winds and sunshine and strife,
    It is here, little sweetheart, embrace me.
    It is here, Oh, sweet lover, come chase me,
    It is here, and the world is a place we
  Will sing in and cling in thro' life.

THEO. GIFT.

I WANDERED lonely as a cloud
　　That floats on high o'er vales and hills,
　When all at once I saw a crowd,
A host of golden Daffodils;
Beside the lake, beneath the trees,
Fluttering and dancing in the breeze.

Continuous as the stars that shine
　　And twinkle on the milky way,
They stretched in never-ending line
　　Along the margin of a bay:
Ten thousand saw I at a glance,
Tossing their heads in sprightly dance.

The waves beside them danced, but they
　　Out-did the sparkling waves in glee:
A poet could not but be gay
　　In such a jocund company;
I gazed—and gazed—but little thought
What wealth the show to me had brought.

For oft, when on my couch I lie
　　In vacant or in pensive mood,
They flash upon that inward eye
　　Which is the bliss of solitude,
And then my heart with pleasure fills,
And dances with the Daffodils.

　　　　　　　　　WORDSWORTH.

The dry leaves
Are lifted by the grass, and so I know
That Nature from her delicate ear hath caught
The dropping of the velvet foot of Spring.

N. P. WILLIS.

V.

*A*FTER April, when May follows
  And the white-throat builds, and all the swallows!
    Hark, where my blossomed pear tree in the hedge
Leans to the field and scatters on the clover
Blossoms and dew drops—at the bent sprays edge—
  That's the wise thrush he sings each song twice over;
Lest you should think he never could recapture
The first fine careless rapture!

ROBERT BROWNING.

VI.

GLAD is the task of hoeing the wheat,
 And wondering who the bread shall eat!
  Perhaps some poet with bay-crowned brow
May eat of the wheat we are hoeing now!
Perhaps it may go to make firm and strong
The arm of the hero to slay the wrong!
It will do its work, and we help it to spring,
Though others may work at the harvesting.

Glad is the task of helping to birth
The blessed fruits of the bounteous earth;
And glad the task of helping to raise
The present's fruit for the coming days!
Sow good—and tend it with steadfast care
And beyond all dreams shall the fruit be fair!
What matter—you helped the fruits to bring—
If you fall asleep ere the harvesting?

E. NESBIT.

SPRING (LOOKING FOR A YOUNG WIFE)

VII.

VER lilies stood up in a row,
 Tall sentinels of state,
Nodding their heads as the little feet
 Pattered down to the gate;
The rose threw down a shower of leaves
 Over her yellow hair,
And the eglantine slyly slipped a rope
 And caught her unaware.

Sudden and sweet a robin sang
 From a milk-white hawthorn bush,
And far away, like a voice in a dream,
 Carolled a building thrush.
A flash of white in the golden air,
 A magpie flitted across,
And bees were humming their drowsy tune
 Over the thymy moss.

Daisies curled in their snowy frills,
 Silvering the grassy lane,
Wooed the small fingers to pluck and weave
 Their pearls in a fringed chain:
A field-mouse peeped with his diamond eyes
 From some waving ribbon grass,
And a squirrel climbed the chestnut tree
 To see our darling pass.

A wandering wind, that had gathered
    The secrets of all the flowers,
Chased through the shadow and sunlight
    This restless baby of ours;
Afar in the green wood's hollow
    A cuckoo proclaimed the Spring,
But our bird's voice was the sweetest
    That day of thanksgiving.

C. BROOKE.

VIII.

*T*HE small birds twitter,
    The lake doth glitter,
  The green field sleeps in the sun;
  The oldest and youngest
  Are at work with the strongest:
  The cattle are grazing,
  Their heads never raising:
There are forty feeding like one!

  Like an army defeated,
  The snow hath retreated,
  And now doth fare ill
  On the top of the bare hill;
The plough-boy is whooping—anon—anon:
  There's joy in the mountains;
  There's life in the fountains;
  Small clouds are sailing,
  Blue sky prevailing;
The rain is over and gone!

WORDSWORTH.

Small clouds are sailing. Blue sky prevailing:

UNDER the thorntree laugh and lie,
   Up on the thorntree sing and swing!
There 'll be Springs a many as years go by
But never again this self same Spring.

IX

KISS me, sweetheart, the Spring
is here,
And Love is Lord of you
and me,
The blue-bells beckon each
passing bee,
The wild wood laughs to the
flowered year,
There is no bird in brake or brere
But to his little mate sings he:
"Kiss me, sweetheart, the Spring is here,
And Love is Lord of you and me!"
The blue sky laughs out sweet and clear,
The missel-thrush upon the tree
Pipes for mere gladness, loud and free,
And I go singing to my dear:
"Kiss me, sweetheart, the Spring is here,
And Love is Lord of you and me."

Summer

HE evening comes, the fields are still,
The tinkle of the thirsty rill,
Unheard all day, ascends again;
Deserted is the half-mown plain,
Silent the swaths! the ringing wain,
  The mowers' cry, the dogs' alarms,
  All housed within the sleeping farm!
  The business of the day is done,
  The last-left haymaker is gone.
  And from the thyme upon the height,
  And from the elder-blossom white
And pale dog-roses
              in the hedge,
And from the mint-plant
      in the sedge,

In puffs of balm the night-air blows
The perfume which the day foregoes.
And on the pure horizon far,
See, pulsing with the first-born star,
The liquid sky above the hill!
The evening comes, the fields are still.

MATTHEW ARNOLD.

II.

*I*T is the hour when from the boughs
  The nightingale's high note is heard,
It is the hour when lover's vows
Seem sweet in every whisper'd word;
And gentle winds, and waters near
Make music to the lonely ear.

BYRON.

III
SONG.

HERE be you going, you Devon maid?
   And what have ye there in the basket?
Ye tight little fairy, just fresh from the dairy,
   Will ye give me some cream if I ask it?

I love your hills and I love your dales,
   And I love your flocks a-bleating;
But oh, on the heather to lie together,
   With both our hearts a-beating!

I'll put your basket all safe in a nook;
   Your shawl I'll hang on a willow,
And we will sigh in the daisy's eye,
   And kiss on a grass-green pillow.

KEATS.

IV.

THERE is a singing in the Summer air,
   The blue and brown moths flutter o'er the grass,
   The stubble bird is creaking in the wheat,
And perch'd upon the honeysuckle hedge
Pipes the green linnet.   Oh, the golden world!
The stir of life on every blade of grass,
The motion and the joy on every bough,
The glad feast every where, for things that love
The sunshine, and for things that love the shade.

R. BUCHANAN.

In Summertime.

V.

WEET is my love so sweet,
   The leaves that, fold on fold,
Swathe up the odours of the rose,
   Less sweetness hold.

VI.

THE FLOWER'S LOT.

'MONG Summer's babes I saw a rose one day,
   In the beginning of its flowery lease,
  With purple cheek, lapped in the bud it lay,
And dreamt but of its innocence and peace.

"Thou pretty floweret, wake, thine eye lift up,
   With life's sweet lot thyself to satisfy,"
Said, fluttering over leaf and flower-cup,
   The wanton, gold-besprinkled butterfly.

"See, dark and poor appears thy dwelling slight,
   As reft of joy thy heart is beating there;
Here gladness liveth, gloweth day's broad light,
   And here await thee love and kisses fair."

Upon the floweret's soul the speech did tell,
   Soon to the flatterer she her mouth lay bare.
The butterfly then kissed her; —bade farewell!
   And to fresh rosebuds swiftly did repair.

RUNEBERG.
Translated by Magnusson and Palmer

VII

MY Luve's like a red, red rose
    That's newly sprung in June:
O my Luve's like the melodie
    That's sweetly played in tune.
As fair art thou, my bonnie lass,
    So deep in luve am I;
And I will luve thee still, my Dear,
    Till a' the seas gang dry:

Till a' the seas gang dry, my Dear,
    And the rocks melt wi' the sun;
I will luve thee still, my Dear,
    While the sands o' life shall run.
And fare thee weel, my only Luve!
    And fare thee weel a while!
And I will come again, my Luve,
    Tho' it were ten thousand mile.

BURNS.

Fair when the corn fields grow warm

Sweet are the lanes and the hedges —
the fields made red with the clover

VIII.

SWEET are the lanes and the hedges—
        the fields made red with the clover,
  With tall field-sorrel, and daisies,
        and golden buttercups glowing,
Sweet is the way through the woods
        where at sundown maiden and lover
  Linger by stile and by bank
        where wild clematis is growing;
Fair is our world when the dew and the dawn
        thrill the half opened roses,
Fair when the corn fields grow warm
        with poppies in noonlight gleaming.
  Fair through the long afternoon,
        when hedges and hay-fields lie dreaming,
Fair as in lessening light the last convolvulus closes.
  Scent of geranium and musk,
        that in cottage windows run riot:
  Breath from the grass that is down
        in the meadows each side the highway;
Slumberous hush of the churchyard
        where we some day may lie quiet,
  Murmuring wind through the leaves
        bent over the meadows by way;
Deeps of cool shadow, and gleams of light
        in high elm-tops shining.
  Such peace in the dim green brake
        as the town save in dreams knows never!

                      E. NESBIT

Gather
ye Rosebuds
while ye may.

IX.

*G*ATHER ye rosebuds while ye may,
 Old Time is still a-flying,
And this same flower
        that smiles to-day,
    To-morrow will be dying.

Then be not coy, but use your time,
    And while ye may, go marry,
For having lost but once your prime,
    You may for ever tarry.

                    HERRICK.

SUMMERS LEASE.

X.

*R*OUGH winds do shake the darling buds of May,
    And Summer's lease hath all too short a date.
      Sometime too hot the eye of heaven shines,
And often is his gold complexion dimm'd
And every fair from fair sometime declines,
By chance, or nature's changing course, untrimm'd
But thy eternal summer shall not fade,
Nor lose possession of that fair thou owest;
Nor shall death brag thou wander'st in his shade
When in eternal lines to time thou growest.

                        SHAKESPEARE.

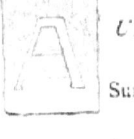AUTUMN clouds are flying, flying
    O'er the waste of blue;
Summer flowers are dying, dying,
    Late so lovely new.
Labouring wains are slowly rolling
    Home with winter grain;
Holy bells are slowly tolling
    Over buried men.

Goldener lights set noon a-sleeping,
    Like an afternoon;
Colder airs come creeping, creeping,
    After sun and moon;
And the leaves, all tired of blowing
    Cloud like o'er the sun,
Change to sunset-colours, knowing
    That their day is done.

              GEORGE MACDONALD.

II.

NOT Spring, too lavish of her bud and leaf,
 But Autumn with sad eyes and brow austere
  When woods once thick with green are thin and sere,
  And leaden skies weep their exhaustless grief.
Spring is so much too bright, so much too brief,
  Since in one's heart is Autumn all the year,
  Least sad when the wide pastures are most drear
And the last field is robbed of the last sheaf.

For when the plough goes down the brown wet field
 A delicate doubtful throb of hope is ours—
What if this coming Spring at last should yield
 Joy,—with her too profuse unasked-for flowers?
Not all our Springs if common-place and pain
Have taught us how that Autumn hope is vain.

III

FALLING leaf and fading tree,
Lines of white on a sullen sea,
Shadows rising on you and me.
The swallows are making them ready to fly,
Wheeling out on a wintry sky.
Good-bye, Summer! Good-bye! good-bye!

IV.

*W*HAT wildness dost thou give the scene,
  Long trailing bramble of the waste,
  With thorn or furze-bush interlaced,
 And broad-leaved fern let in between
 So close, there's scarcely room to pass.

Many such tangling spots we know,
 With patches of short velvet grass,
Where heath and nodding blue-bells grow,
The bullace and the dark blue sloe,
And gushing bramble-berries glow.
   All hung with rime
   In autumn time,
   And to and fro
   They ever go,
When the leaf-stripping breezes blow.

their own is
as hazel-nut,
and
sweeter than
the kernels

V.

FLOATING, floating, from dawn to dusk
    Till the pearly twilight dies,
  And the mists float up from the sapphire sea
    And cloud all the sapphire skies.
  Floating, floating, while golden stars
Seem to float in a sea over-head,
And stormy lights from a sea below
  Glow orange and purple and red.
        Till we seem floating out of the sea of life,
        The tempest of passion the stormwinds of strife.
        Out into strange mysterious space
        Till God shall find us a landing place.

Drifting, drifting, to lands unkown
  From a world of love and care,
Drifting away to a home untried,
  And a heart that is waiting there.
O ship sail swiftly, oh waters deep
  Bear me safe to that haven unknown
Safe to the tender love that waits
    To be for ever my own.
        Till we drift away from the sea of life,
        The tempest of passion, the stormwinds of strife.
        Out to a haven, out to a shore,
        Where life is love for evermore.
                                CARIS BROOKE.

Floating floating from dawn to dusk
Till the pearly twilight dies

A LULLABY.

OH! WANDERING wind, I pray thee fold thy wings,
   The whispering trees are calling thee to rest,
   The sky grows dim, the noisy birds are still,
And softly sleeps my baby at my breast.

Oh! restless sea, whose waters wan and cold,
   Fret the brown rocks with angry moon-white crest
Hush them, I pray to little lapping waves,
   For softly sleeps my baby at my breast.

Oh! guardian stars, half hid by fleecy cloudlets,
   Your watch-fires now I pray make manifest,
No other light have we within the chamber,
   Where softly sleeps my baby at my breast.

Oh! Lord of earth, and sea, and stars, and heaven,
   Come to our home to-night, and be our guest,
So in the darkness, which is as thy shadow,
   Shall softly sleep my baby at my breast.

                                        CARIS BROOKE

Where softly sleeps my baby at my breast

VII.

O COME at last, to whom the Spring-tide's hope
　　Looked for through blossoms what hast thou for me?
　Green grows the grass upon the dewy slope
Beneath thy gold-hung grey leavé apple tree,
Moveless, e'en as the Autumn fain would be,
　　That shades its sad eyes from the rising sun,
　　And weeps at eve because the day is done.

What image will thou give me, Autumn morn,
　To make thy pensive sweetness more complete?
What tale, ne'er to be told, of folk unborn?
　What images of grey-clad damsels sweet,
　　Shall cross thy sward with dainty noiseless feet?
　　What nameless shamefast longings made alive,
　　Soft-eyed September, will thy sad heart give?

Look long, O longing eyes, and look in vain!
　Long idly, aching heart, and yet be wise;
And hope no more for things to come again
　Which thou beheldest once with careless eyes!
　　Like a new wakened man thou art, who tries
　　To dream again the dream that made him glad,
　　When in his arms his loving love he had.

W　MORRIS.

TO AUTUMN.

SEASON of mist and mellow fruitfulness!
    Close bosom-friend of the maturing sun;
Conspiring with him how to load and bless
    With fruit the vines that round
        the thatch-eaves run;
To bend with apples the moss'd cottage-trees,
    And fill all fruit with ripeness to the core;
To swell the gourd, and plump the hazel shells
    With a sweet kernel; to set budding more
And still more, later flowers for the bees,
Until they think warm days will never cease;
    For Summer has o'er-brimm'd their clammy cells.

Where are the songs of Spring? Ay, where are they?
    Think not of them,—thou hast thy music too.
While barrèd clouds bloom the soft-dying day
    And touch the stubble-plains with rosy hue;
Then in a wailful choir the small gnats mourn
    Among the river sallows, born aloft
Or sinking as the light wind lives or dies;
    And full-grown lambs loud bleat from hilly bourn;
Hedge-crickets sing, and now with treble soft
The red-breast whistles from a garden-croft,
    And gathering swallows twitter in the skies.

KEATS.

IX.

*T*HE sea is at ebb
   and the sound of her
      utmost word
Is soft as the least wave's lapse
   in a still, small reach.

A. C. SWINBURNE.

*O*N either side the river lie
   Long fields of barley and of rye,
That clothe the wold and meet the sky.

Tennyson.

. . . . Reapers, reaping early,
In among the bearded barley.

Tennyson.

. . . Autumn laying here and there,
A fiery finger on the leaves.

Tennyson.

A GOOD-BYE

HOW soon the ocean of dim distance rolls
   Wave upon wave between our parted souls;
      How little to each other now are we,
And once how much I dreamed
                  we two might be,
I, who now stand with eyes
                  undimmed and dry,
         To say good-bye.

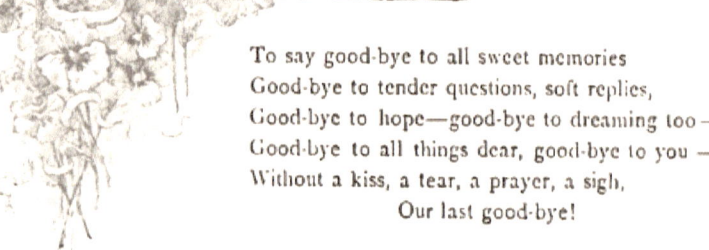

To say good-bye to all sweet memories
Good-bye to tender questions, soft replies,
Good-bye to hope—good-bye to dreaming too—
Good-bye to all things dear, good-bye to you—
Without a kiss, a tear, a prayer, a sigh,
            Our last good-bye!

I had no chains to bind you with at all,
No grace to charm, no beauty to enthrall;
No power to hold your eyes with mine, and make
Your heart on fire with longing for my sake,
Till all the yearning passed into one cry —
         "Love—*not* good-bye!"

Ah! no, I had no strength like that you know,
Yet my worst weakness was to love you so,
So much too well—so much too well—or ill—
Yet even that might have been pardoned still,
It would have been, had I been you, you I—
        But now good-bye.

How soon the bitter follows on the sweet!
Could I not chain your fancy's flying feet?
Could I not hold your soul, to make you play
To-morrow in the key of yesterday?
Dear, do you dream that I would stoop to try?
        Ah no! good-bye!

                                        E. NESBIT.

OCTOBER.

EFORE the Winter holds the streams ice-bound,
  And shrouds the sky, as with a veil, in gloom,
Once more we hear the song of birds resound,
  And see the sweet, last rose of Summer bloom.

In chill October we may ye behold
  Nature arrayed in gorgeous livery;
Warm purple sunsets, leaves of glittering gold,
  Have all the charm of splendour doomed to die.

Thou know'st, my soul, that beauty cannot last;
  Yet, in despite of this sad month of sighs,
Hope once again, forget the dim, dark past,
  And try to snatch the moment as it flies.

Build yet another castle in the air;
  Reck not of Winter, knocking at the gate,
Whose ruthless rake alas, knows not to spare
  Our shattered hopes, the dear dead leaves of fate.

C. MAINWARING.

XII.

HEN all the world is old lad,
　And all the trees are brown,
And all the sport is stale lad,
　And all the wheels run down;
Creep home and take your place there
　The spent and maimed among,
God grant you find one face there
　You loved when all was young.

XIII.

LOVE! turn from the unchanging sea, and gaze
   Down these grey slopes upon the year grown old,
   A-dying, 'mid the Autumn scented haze,
That lieth in the hollow on the wold,
Where the wind-bitten ancient elms enfold
Grey church, long barn, orchard and red-roofed stead
Wrought in dead days for men a long while dead.

Come down, O Love; may not our hands still meet
Since still we live to-day, forgetting June,
Forgetting May, deeming October sweet—
O hearken, hearken, through the afternoon
The gray tower sings a strange old tinkling tune!
Sweet, sweet and sad, the toiling years last breath
Too satiate of life to strive with death.

And we, too, will it not be soft and kind,
That rest from life, from patience, and from pain—
That rest from bliss we know not when we find—
That rest from love that ne'er the end can gain?
Hark! how the tune swells that erewhile did wane;
Look up, love! ah, cling close and never move!
How can I have enough of life and love?

W. MORRIS.

Snowdrifts

Winter

WHEN icicles hang by the wall,
  And Dick the shepherd blows his nail,
And Tom bears logs into the hall,
  And milk comes frozen home in pail,
    *   *   *   *   *
When all aloud the wind doth blow,
And birds sit brooding in the snow.

SHAKSPEARE.

THAT time of year thou may'st in me behold
  When yellow leaves, or none, or few, do hang
Upon those boughs which shake against the cold,
  Bare ruin'd choirs, where late the sweet birds sang.

SHAKSPEARE.

II.

*T*HE Winter time,
  With snow and rime,
    Has sprung from sunburnt Autumn's breast;
And in her lap
She holds, mayhap,
A Spring of all the Springs the best.

So may thy soul
Not lose control
Of joy, but still be pure and strong,
All Winter comes
From harvest-homes
Of peace, and draws the Spring along

A Gracious Hand

III.

*E*VER so late in the year will come
    Many a red Geranium,
        And chrysanthemums up to November;
Then the Winter has overtaken them all—
The fogs and the rains begin to fall,
And the flowers, after running their races,
Are weary, and shut up their little faces
And under the ground they go to sleep.
Is it very far down? Yes, ever so deep.

LILLIPUT LEVEE.

DEAR gracious hand that casts upon the snow
Food to your birds who to your feet fly low—
Cast me some crumb of kindness, since you know
I starve to death because I want you so.

E. NESBIT

IV.

*O*UTSIDE, the world with snow is white,
But all our home is warm and bright
With firelight's ruddy gleam and glow,
And mother's love as well, you know.—
And that's why home's the dearest place
Because of mother's darling face.

Oh! mother dear, on Christmas day,
It did seem hard to be away;
The pudding and the fat mince-pies,
Somehow, seemed not so very nice —
Though every one was kind, we knew
That what we wanted so was you.

And mother has a present here
—She said she had—for our new Year.
What is it lying on her lap,
That fluffy woolly shawls enwrap?
Oh—Billy, Dolly, Madge—look here
It *is* a little Baby dear!

How good it was of it to come
Just when we were expected home!
This is the loveliest New Year's day!
We little thought when far away
That mother, whom we left alone,
Had a new Baby of her own.

Did Angels bring it through the snow?
Or did it in the garden grow?
It's too cold in the garden yet
For snowdrop or for violet;
But Christmas roses bloom—who knows?
Baby may be a Christmas-rose!

I think Christ sent it, made it grow—
He knew that we should love it so;
For he was once a Baby too,
And used to cry, and laugh, and coo
Into his mother's face for hours,
A little Baby, just like ours!

                              E. Nesbit.

In a drear-nighted December,
        Too happy, happy brook,
    Thy bubblings ne'er remember
Apollo's summer look;

        But with a sweet
                forgetting,
    They stay their crystal   .
                fretting,
    Never, never petting
        About the frozen time.

V.

*I*N a drear-nighted December,
 Too happy, happy tree,
 Thy branches ne'er remember
Their green felicity :
The north cannot undo them,
With a sleety whistle through them ;
Nor frozen thawings glue them
 From budding at the prime.

In a drear-nighted December,
 Too happy, happy brook,
Thy bubblings ne'er remember
 Apollo's summer look ;
But with a sweet forgetting,
They stay their crystal fretting,
Never, never petting
 About the frozen time.

Ah! would 'twere so with many
 A gentle girl and boy!
But were there ever any
 Writhed not at passed joy?
To know the change and feel it,
When there is none to heal it,
Nor numbed sense to steal it,
 Was never said in rhyme.

KEATS.

Novembe

VI.

*O*UTSIDE the garden
  The wet skies harden;
    The gates are barred on
The Summer side;
"Shut out the flower time,
Sunbeam and shower time,
Make room for our time!"
    Wild winds have cried.

Green once and cheery,
The woods, worn weary,
Sigh as the dreary
    Weak sun goes home;
A great wind grapples
The wave, and dapples
  The dead green floor of the sea with foam.
                    SWINBURNE.

                The chill
November dawns and dewy-glooming downs,
The gentle shower, the smell of dying leaves,
And the low moan of leaden-coloured seas.
                    TENNYSON.

is heigh ho

unto the

green holly

VII.

*T*HE cold earth slept below;
　　Above the cold sky shone;
　　And all around,
　　　With a chilling sound,
From caves of ice and fields of snow,
The breath of night like death did flow
　　Beneath the sinking moon.

　　　　The wintry hedge was black,
　　　　　The green grass was not seen,
　　　　　　The birds did rest
　　　　　　On the bare thorn's breast,
　　　　Whose roots, beside the pathway track,
　　　　Had bound the folds o'er many a crack,
　　　　　Which the frost had made between.

P. B. SHELLEY

LOVE IN WINTER.

ETWEEN the berried holly-bush
  The blackbird whistled to the thrush,
"Which way did bright-eyed Bella go?
Look, speckle-breast, across the snow.
Are these her dainty tracks I see
That wind beside the shrubbery?"

The throstle picked the berries still:
"No need for looking, yellow-bill,
Young Frank was there an hour ago
Half frozen, waiting in the snow;
His callow beard was white with rime;
'Tchuck, 'tis a merry pairing time!"

"What would you?" twittered in the wren,
"These are the reckless ways of men;
I watched them bill and coo as though
They thought the sign of Spring was snow;
If men but timed their loves as we
'Twould save this inconsistency."

"Nay, gossip," said the robin, "nay,
I like their unreflective way.
Besides, I heard enough to show
Their love is proof against the snow;
'Why wait,' he said, 'why wait for May,
When love can warm a Winter's day?'"

ACSTIN DOBSON

*F*OLIAGE paleth,
   Trees their raiment shed,
    And November gloom prevaileth
    O'er dead flowers' bed.
Snowy drifts their crowns have blighted;
But in hearts whom they delighted;
While the Summer's warmth did still remain,
They revive as memories again.

    Roses flower,
      For a few day's span;
    But outlasts their Summer's hour,
      Thy flower's lease, oh! man?
Fair it shooteth forth and gleameth,
Glows its cheek, its bright eye beameth;
But against its stem a breeze there flies,
And it fades, and stoops, and shrinks, and dies.

Thou, who didst wake me out of earth's dark night,
'Mid thy flower creation make me sprout forth pure and bright,
That though Summer's sun ignore me,
Some kind angels may have for me,
'Mong the memories he from earth shall bear,
One, too, of my quiet blooming there.

RUNEBERG

X.

THE HOPE.

*W*HILE yet the air is keen and no bird sings,
  Nor any vaguest thrills of heart declare
  The presence of the Springtime in the air,
Through the raw dawn the shepherd homeward brings
The warm wite lambs—the little helpless things,
  For shelter, warmth and comfortable care;
  Without his aid how hardly lambs would fare!
How hardly live through Winter's hours to Spring's!

So let me tend and minister apart
  To my new hope, (which someday you shall know.)
  It could not live in January wind
Of your disdain, but when within your heart
  The bud and bloom of tenderness shall grow,
Amid the flowers my hope may welcome find.

E. Nesbit.

WINTER.

*B*ITE, frost, bite!
   You roll up away from the light:
      The blue wood-louse, and the plump dormouse.
And the bees are stilled, and the flies are kill'd,
And you bite far into the heart of the house,
But not into mine.

*F*ULL knee-deep lies the Winter snow,
   And the Winter winds are wearily sighing:
      Toll ye the church-bell sad and low,
For the old year lies a-dying.

TENNYSON.